THE GHOST'S REVENGE

by M. Peschke
illustrated by Brann Garvey

Librarian Reviewer
Diane R. Chen
Library Information Specialist, Hickman Elementary, Nashville, TN
MA in LIS, University of Iowa
BA El Ed & Modern Languages/Chinese, Buena Vista University

Reading Consultant
Mark DeYoung
Classroom Teacher, Edina Public Schools, MN
BA in Elementary Education, Central College
MS in Curriculum & Instruction, University of MN

STONE ARCH BOOKS
Minneapolis   San Diego

Vortex Books are published by Stone Arch Books,
A Capstone Imprint
151 Good Counsel Drive, P.O. Box 669
Mankato, Minnesota 56002
www.capstonepub.com

Library of Congress Cataloging-in-Publication Data
Peschke, M. (Marci)
  The Ghost's Revenge / by M. Peschke; illustrated by Brann Garvey.
  p. cm. — (Vortex Books)
  Summary: The Comanche warrior that Zack has been seeing in
his dreams has begun to appear in real life, and as the line between
his dream world and the real world blurs, the teenager embarks on a
dangerous journey to resolve an old misunderstanding.
  ISBN-13: 978-1-59889-071-6 (hardcover)
  ISBN-10: 1-59889-071-9 (hardcover)
  ISBN-13: 978-1-59889-283-3 (paperback)
  ISBN-10: 1-59889-283-5 (paperback)
  [1. Ghosts—Fiction. 2. Comanche Indians—Fiction. 3. Indians of
North America—Texas—Fiction. 4. Texas—Fiction.] I. Garvey, Brann,
ill. II. Title. III. Series.
PZ7.P441245Gh 2007
[Fic]—dc22   2006007685

Art Director: Heather Kindseth
Graphic Designer: Kay Fraser

Photo Credits
Karon Dubke, cover images
      Printed in the United States of America in Stevens Point, Wisconsin.
                                    042011
                                   006150R

For Joe, Jason, Genny, and Mom
Thanks for all of your love and support

TABLE OF CONTENTS

THE NIGHTMARE

Zack Parker felt as if he were packed in snow. His skin was cold as ice. His body was frozen in fear.

Ink black eyes stared at him. The eyes were surrounded by long black hair swirling around an angry face. The hard mouth was screaming something at Zack. Something he could not understand.

Zack woke up with a jolt.

His heart was racing. He looked around his room. Dirty clothes, cola cans, and video games made a carpet across the floor.

His dog, Doc, lay peacefully snoring in the middle of the mess. The angry face with the long, swirling hair was gone.

Zack sighed and leaned back. As his skin touched the damp, sweaty sheet, he bounced back up and hit his head against the bottom of the bunk overhead. Ouch! The top of his head pounded with pain.

Luckily, he didn't sweat like this every night. Just on certain nights, he thought.

The warrior nights.

CHAPTER 1

A NEW HOBBY

It was a hot Texas summer day, and Zack rode his bike through Johnson City's small town square. He parked at the bike rack and walked over to the drugstore.

He lifted his hand to give a high five to the old wooden Indian statue that stood outside the glass door.

"Zack, can you work the soda fountain today?" Mr. Johnson asked.

"No problemo," Zack answered.

Once behind the counter, he looked up and saw his friends enter the store. Each boy gave the Indian a high five and headed for the soda fountain. Seth, Wes, and Josh all took seats at the counter.

"How's it going?" Josh asked.

"We've got cherry Cokes on special for a buck," said Zack.

The three nodded, and Zack poured the Cokes, adding a shot of cherry syrup to each glass.

"Y'all know much about Indians?" Zack asked, placing the Cokes on the counter. He looked at his three best friends and waited for an answer.

"Why are you asking us about Indians?" Wes said. "You know everything we know, since we learned it from Ms. Butler in fourth grade. Right?

"Just a new hobby." Zack wiped the marble counter with a soapy rag.

"Are you thinking of collecting arrow heads or something?" Seth asked.

"Uh, yeah," said Zack. He hated lying to his friends, but they wouldn't understand about his nightmare.

"Buck Thomas has about a hundred of them," Wes said. "Talk to him. He's the closest thing we've got to an expert around here."

"Have you been over to the library?" Josh asked.

"No, but that's a good idea," Zack said.

"I have an idea," Seth said. He tapped a spoon on the counter. "When you get off work, we could go over to Llano and check out the museum."

Zack said, "I have to work until closing."

Seth shrugged.

Josh headed for the door. "Later," he said.

Seth and Wes followed him.

Zack watched as they slapped the hand of the statue on the way out. The face of the wooden Indian looked so harmless and friendly. The rest of the day all Zack could think about was the angry, savage face of the fierce warrior who haunted his dreams.

Chapter 2

THE RIVER

When Zack was finished with his shift at the drug store, the guys picked him up, and they headed down to the river for a swim.

The dirt road snaked along with hardly any signs of civilization.

Soon they came to a pale green river surrounded by white limestone rock formations, cactus, and a few oak and mesquite trees here and there.

The river was cold and felt great on the hot summer day. Each of the guys took turns swinging out over the water on a knotted rope that hung from a bent oak tree. Then they would shout something. Wes shouted, "Jaguars rule!" then swung out far, jumping into the water with a neat splash.

Seth yelled, "Nerds rule!" and swung out only a short way before landing painfully on his stomach.

"Belly flop," they all screamed loudly and laughed.

Josh went next. Skipping any words, he just swung out, farted loudly, and landed. The others yelled, "Stink bomb!"

"Dang, Josh, what did you eat this morning?" Seth demanded.

"Hey it's my turn!" Zack announced. He yelled, "Geronimo!"

Zack made a perfect landing, but when his head came up he was screaming in pain. The water turned blood red around him.

"My foot!" he shouted. "Somebody get my shirt from the truck!"

The guys all looked surprised. The bottom of the river was smooth at this spot and allowed them to go barefoot.

Seth raced to the truck to grab Zack's t-shirt. Painfully, Zack limped from the water. Josh took the shirt from Seth and pressed it hard against his friend's foot to stop the bleeding.

"Ouch!" Zack cried.

Wes was still treading water. "What did you hit?" he asked, peering into the river.

"Not sure," Zack called back.

Wes dove down and felt along the bottom of the river.

When Wes broke the surface of the water he was holding a small, sharp object.

"It looks like you just started that arrowhead collection," he said.

* * *

Later that afternoon, Zack made a visit to the Johnson City Public Library.

Ms. June Rhodes, the librarian, did not wear glasses or shush people in the library. Zack liked her. She smiled kindly at him as he came in.

When Zack said he was interested in reading about Native Americans, she pointed him to the corner of the library where the 900s were shelved. Zack pulled out several books and sat down at a table.

He carefully removed the arrowhead from his pocket and unfolded the paper towel around it.

According to one of the books, his was a fairly common arrowhead that could have been made and used by many different tribes or bands of Native Americans.

Zack was just about to close the book when his eye caught a small portrait of a warrior on the bottom of the page.

He pulled the book closer and looked carefully at the warrior. The man wore a tan shirt, tan leggings, and fringed moccasins. They were probably made of buckskin, Zack thought.

The man's wild black hair, angry face, and intense eyes made Zack shiver. His mom would say a sudden chill like that meant a ghost had stepped on his grave.

He looked at the picture again.

The man was on horseback and wore feathers in his hair.

A large claw hung from a leather cord around the man's neck.

The object that stopped Zack cold was the long spear that seemed to be pointing right out of the book.

Right at him.

Chapter 3

DREAM HORSE

Thud, thud, thud!

Zack heard the steady pounding of hooves. He woke up, but was he dreaming? It must be a dream.

The dirty desert floor spread out around him. In the distance, he could see the warrior on horseback coming closer and closer.

He scrambled to get up. His brain was ordering him to move, and move fast.

He began to run, but with each step he sank into the sand and the warrior rode closer. He was so close that Zack could feel the horse breathing against his back.

Suddenly, Zack stumbled and fell. The horse reared up. Legs and hooves stretched over Zack's head. Zack raised his arms across his face and rolled to the left.

Then he heard a terrifying scream. Zack flew out of his bunk and crashed against his closet door. His heart was racing, and he was dripping with sweat.

"Just a dream, just another dream," he muttered. It was hard to get the words out. He was breathing hard, too hard. He had a stomach cramp just like the time his coach made him run sprints and he puked in the grass when he was finished.

He slowly sat up.

Zack looked around the room. Things seemed normal, but where was Doc?

Then he heard a whimper. Doc was backed against the wall under the bed.

Zack leaned over, still gasping, and called, "Come on, boy." He held out his hand, and Doc wiggled to the edge of the mattress but would not come out from under the bed until Zack opened the door to let him out. It was really sad when your bad dreams were scaring your dog, too.

Zack went into the bathroom, rinsed his face with cool water, and patted it dry with a blue towel.

In the mirror, he could see his green eyes. They were red and bloodshot.

Had he been screaming, or did the warrior yell some kind of war cry just as his horse was about to crush the boy under him?

As he crawled back into bed, Zack heard pounding again. "Zack, let's roll!" his mom yelled. "Do you want to go with me to San Antonio or not?"

"Yeah, I do," he replied quietly, pretending like he was still asleep.

"Okay. Get ready. You've got ten minutes," his mom said. "And Doc needs to be fed."

Zack heard a long whine from the direction of the door. It was Doc.

"Here, boy," Zack called. He got up and opened the door. But Doc wouldn't come into the room.

Then Zack noticed that his Gameboy was smashed to bits on the floor. He bent over and looked closer. It was completely crushed. Some pieces of it were a fine plastic powder. Someone, or something, had destroyed his Gameboy on purpose.

By the time he got dressed and wandered into the kitchen, something smelled terrific. His mom had made his favorite, pecan pancakes and bacon. She was drinking coffee and reading the paper.

After he ate, he cleared the dishes, rinsed, and put them in the dishwasher. His mom told him their first stop would be the bank, for a little spending money. That gave Zack an idea. "Can I take some money out of my savings account?" he asked.

"What do you plan to use the money for?" his mom asked, looking confused.

Zack knew he needed a new Gameboy, but there was no way he could logically explain it. Even he didn't understand what happened to the old one. It was crazy, but he thought a horse had stepped on it.

Chapter 4

QUANAH PARKER

After stopping at the bank, and then at the Quick-E Mart to fill the old green Escort wagon with gas, Zack's mom turned on to Highway Ten, which would lead them into San Antonio. It would take about two hours to get there.

"Mom, can we talk?" Zack asked.

She turned off the radio and said, "Sure. What do you want to talk about?"

Zack quickly replied, "Indians."

"The Cleveland Indians?" His mom sounded confused.

"No, I mean Native Americans."

"You mean like the Cherokee, Comanche, and Hopi tribes?" she asked.

Zack nodded. It seemed like his mom remembered everything from the World Book Encyclopedia she had as a kid. She started talking. Zack listened and watched the passing scenery through the car window. He could see clouds shaped like a horse, a claw, and a mountain. Today the sky was really blue.

Suddenly his mom said something that shocked him. She said, "The Parkers are related to a famous Comanche, you know."

He sat up in the car seat and faced her. "Why didn't you ever tell me that before?" he demanded.

"It never came up before. Besides, it may not be true," she answered. "It's just an old story Grandpa Parker used to tell your dad and Uncle Jack," she continued.

She told him that Grandpa Parker had said they were related to the famous Comanche chief Quanah Parker, and that Quanah never lost a battle to the white man.

"Did Grandpa Parker have any proof that we're related to the chief?" Zack interrupted. "Did we save any of Grandpa Parker's papers? Who has them now? How about his other stuff? Is it in the attic?" he shouted.

"Slow down, Zack," she said. "Uncle Jack has Grandpa Parker's papers, and there might still be some of his things in the attic." Zack was about to ask another fifty questions when his mom turned the car into the mall's parking lot.

* * *

It wasn't until several days later that Zack worked up the nerve to call his Uncle Jack. His Aunt Dianne said he would have to call back next week, because his uncle was working offshore on an oil rig.

On Sunday night Zack called the guys on his cell phone and asked them to come over and help him dig through the attic.

When the guys arrived, they each lifted themselves up into the cramped, dusty space.

"What are we looking for up here?" Wes asked.

"Anything about Native Americans, or any papers that might have been my grandpa's," Zack directed. He told them that he might be related to Quanah Parker, a famous Comanche chief.

Josh said, "No way!"

Zack grabbed a box and began digging through it. A bunch of moth-eaten clothes were stuffed inside. He put it aside to throw in the trash.

Wes was going through a box of books. "Hey, I may have something here," he said. "Here's a bunch of books about the Old West. Some could be about Indian tribes."

Each of the guys grabbed a handful, and they began leafing through the books. A lot of the books were about the early days of the western frontier and famous people like Billy the Kid.

An open book was lying on the dirty floor. "What's this?" Wes asked. He bent down to pick it up.

The book was titled *Chiefs of Many Nations*. At the open page, Wes found an old photograph lying loose.

Since it was after nine o'clock and the attic was getting dark, the boys decided to take the book and the picture downstairs, where they could get a better look.

The boys sat down at the kitchen table. Zack pulled the picture closer while Seth examined the book.

Finally, Seth said, "The only clue here is one bent page."

He turned the book so everyone could read the page describing a chief named Peta Nocona. He just happened to be Quanah Parker's father.

"This is definitely a clue, "Zack said.

"Maybe the chief in the picture is Peta Nocona," Josh said.

"No, I don't think so, " said Seth.

He had read that even though there were no pictures of the chief, the descriptions of Nocona in the book talked about him being a physical giant.

"What else does it say?" asked Zack.

Seth told them that Nocona's name meant "He Who Travels and Returns." His birth date was unknown.

Nocona led raids with a band of Indians called the Noconies, and in 1836, he took Cynthia Ann Parker captive.

"Parker?" said Zack.

"'Some people believe the chief died at the Pease River battle in 1860, but others, including Quanah, cast doubt on this report,'" read Seth.

Zack stared closely at the old, wrinkled photograph.

The Indian chief was wearing the clothes of a white man, and was wrapped in an Indian blanket. He was sitting down. Feathers bristled from his long braids.

Zack turned the photo over. On the back two names were written. QUANAH PARKER? and CYNTHIA ANN PARKER.

"This has to be Grandpa Parker's writing," Zack said. "He only wrote in capital letters."

"What does it mean?" Wes asked.

Zack laid the photograph back in the middle of the table. "I'm not sure yet, but I plan to find out."

Chapter 5

STITCHES

That night, Zack was wiped out after spending the evening cleaning the attic. He was sound asleep when his mom passed by his door and flipped off the lights.

He was thirsty. He was hot. He was running again. With each step he sank into sand, but he continued to run. Behind him he heard the distant pounding of hoof beats. Maybe he could get away before the warrior chief could catch him.

Zack pushed himself harder, plodding through the sandy ground. A hundred feet ahead, he saw a large group of rocks.

Safety!

When he turned his head, he could see the horse behind him. The warrior rode bareback, his jet-black braids flying in the wind. He no longer held the horse's mane, but sat up tall, holding an outstretched bow and arrow.

Zack didn't want to look at the warrior's face, but he couldn't help it. There was hatred in the man's dark eyes.

The bow pulled tight, and the arrow was set free, speeding toward him in a gentle arc.

Zack reached the rocks.

A piercing, hot pain shot through his body. He heard himself scream. Tears ran down his cheeks. He began to shake.

Looking down, Zack could see the arrow buried in his foot. Without thinking, he grabbed the shaft of the arrow and yanked it out of his body.

Then the pain grew worse. He felt his head spinning. Then he passed out.

The dream was over.

Slowly, Zack woke up.

He felt something sticky at the foot of his bed. Opening one eye, he shifted to his side and looked down at his feet. The bed sheets were bright red.

He began to scream. The gears in his mind were going a hundred miles an hour, trying to make sense of what was happening.

Did the warrior really shoot him with the arrow? It couldn't be true!

Hearing him scream, Zack's mom ran down the hall and threw open his door. She took one look at the blood in his bed and began to scream. Zack took one look at his mom in her lime-green face cream and let out another yell.

"What happened?" she cried out, running toward the bed.

Zack pulled his feet out of the sheets and swung them over the side of the bed. They were both bloody. He pulled up the foot that was sore to take a better look.

Kneeling down, his mom looked at the foot. "This wound needs stitches," she said in a panicked voice.

After quickly cleaning the wound she ran to her room to pull on jeans and a shirt. They piled into the station wagon and sped off to Doc Barnes's office.

Johnson City was so small that it didn't have a hospital, or even an emergency clinic, but Doc Barnes still made house calls and never minded the occasional emergency.

Once the doctor got them inside, he examined Zack's foot. After asking several questions, Doc Barnes said Zack must have opened his old wound from the river. Stitches weren't needed for the wound.

Doc Barnes cleaned it, bandaged it up, and gave Zack a tetanus shot. Zack didn't like the shot, but he decided it was a lot better than getting stitches.

An hour later, after they had returned home, Zack was resting on the couch with his sore foot on top of a pile of fluffy brown pillows.

His mother was angry when he told her about stepping on the arrowhead at the river.

"You should have told me right away," she said. "That could have been infected."

Zack knew that the wound on his foot had been completely healed. There was no reason it should have started bleeding again. No normal reason, anyway.

He also knew that the dreams were getting worse. Zack was still thinking about the dreams when his cell phone rang.

"This is your Uncle Jack," came the voice from the phone.

Zack told his uncle he was just the person he wanted to hear. "Uncle Jack, do you remember Grandpa Parker telling a story about being related to Quanah Parker?"

Uncle Jack exploded with a booming laugh. "Many times, Zack, but I never really believed it." He paused.

Thoughtfully, he went on, "Your grandpa did a lot of research into the family background, though. As far as I know he could never find any true connection between the Parkers and Quanah Parker."

"Bummer!" said Zack.

"Why the sudden interest in the old stories?" asked Uncle Jack.

"Just curious," said Zack. "No reason."

"Tell you what, sport. I'll send Grandpa Parker's papers to you tomorrow by UPS, " Uncle Jack offered.

Zack could hardly believe his ears.

* * *

One late afternoon a few days later, Zack heard a truck drive up to the house. By the time Zack reached the front door, the truck was gone.

A brown box was sitting on the porch swing. Zack limped over and picked it up. It had been sent from Houston, Texas.

Zack pulled out his pocketknife. He cut the seal carefully, afraid he might accidentally cut some of the papers inside the box. The contents were as disorganized as his bedroom floor. Some papers were bent, others were torn, some were yellow with age.

Zack took the box into the house and started sorting the papers on the kitchen table. In the bottom of the box, he found three ancient family Bibles. He also found some newspaper clippings, mostly notices about funerals, and a torn spiral notebook. There was writing in the notebook, so he guessed it was full of Grandpa Parker's notes.

After pouring a soda into a glass of ice, Zack went outside, sat on the porch swing, and read through the notebook.

It was growing dark, and crickets were chirping when he reached the final page. He saw a note that read, "Call cousin Dorothy Parker." Then there was a phone number.

He glanced at the phone number again and his heart sped up a little. It looked like a Llano County phone number. Suddenly he was filled with excitement. He had a real lead.

Did this Dorothy Parker person still have that same phone number? Was she even still alive? He had to know right away.

Zack rushed inside to get his cell phone. He punched in the numbers. Just as he was about to hit the Send button, he noticed the phone's glowing face.

It was already nine o'clock. Tough break, he thought. His mom would kill him if he called a perfect stranger this late at night. Doc started to whine.

Zack said, "The call will have to wait until the morning, huh, boy?" Zack flipped on the porch light and swung the back door open.

The dog ran out, and Zack called, "Stay in the yard, Doc!" He peered into the darkness, but couldn't see his dog anywhere.

He heard a loud snort. An animal was breathing heavily somewhere in the yard. Doc ran back to the door, his tail tucked between his legs. His big, staring eyes pleaded with Zack.

"What's wrong, Doc?" asked Zack.

Doc looked into the dark yard and started to whimper.

"Get inside, boy," said Zack, quickly opening and shutting the door. He was sure the unseen animal snorting in the darkness was a horse.

Chapter 6

THE BEAR CLAW

The next morning, Zack headed for the kitchen. His bare feet slapped against the wood floor.

His mom was reading the paper. She peered over the top and asked, "What's wrong with Doc? I tried putting him out this morning and he wouldn't go."

Zack shrugged. "He was acting really weird last night, too."

Doc barked. It was almost like he knew they were talking about him.

"Try putting him out now," his mom said.

Zack opened the back door, and Doc rushed out past him. The dog kept barking.

"What's wrong with you, Doc?" asked Zack. He stepped out into the yard and walked over to his frantic pet.

Doc was digging a hole in the hard-packed dirt. "You got a chicken bone down there, Doc?" Zack asked.

Looking down into the hole, Zack could see there was no chicken bone. Instead, a perfectly formed bear claw lay against the reddish dirt.

Zack had seen it before. The leather cord was missing, but other than that, it looked exactly like the claw that hung from the warrior's neck in his dream.

Stunned, the boy sat down on the ground with his mouth hanging open. Zack blinked a few times. Was he awake or still asleep? He stood up slowly. He walked over to the shed, found an empty glass jar, and came back and scooped up the bear claw. Its talons scraped against the jar's sides.

Zack walked into the kitchen. His mom had gone upstairs. He glanced at the clock. It was after eight. Zack grabbed the notebook with Dorothy Parker's phone number in it and anxiously dialed the number.

The phone rang several times, and every time it rang, Zack's stomach felt weird. What would he say if someone answered?

He was about to hang up when a woman's voice said, "Hello?" The voice sounded out of breath. "Is anyone there?"

Zack blurted out a long confusing sentence about Grandpa Parker and relatives and family trees.

"I'm Dorothy Parker, your Grandpa's cousin. You must be Todd and Cathy's boy," she said.

"Yes ma'am, I am," Zack said. "Ms. Parker, have you found anything in your research about your family, I mean our family, that proves we are related to Quanah Parker?"

"First of all, you call me Ms. Dorothy," said the voice. "Ms. Parker sounds so old. Has your Grandpa Parker filled your head with Indian stories?" she asked.

"No, ma'am," Zack replied. Zack explained that he was really serious about finding out about the Parkers. "Ms. Dorothy, I have Grandpa Parker's papers completely sorted already."

Ms. Dorothy said, "Well, that does sound pretty serious! Can you meet me tomorrow at the Llano Museum, at three o'clock?"

"Yes, Ms. Parker. I mean, Ms. Dorothy!" Zack said.

The next afternoon, Zack, Josh, Wes and Seth drove into Llano.

They could see the courthouse rising up like an old gray giant. It was built right in the center of the town square. The Llano County Museum was located in an old house near the river.

Zack repeated the directions Ms. Dorothy had given him.

Moments later, Josh pulled into the parking lot and parked the truck under a mesquite tree. Zack jumped out and hurried inside the building.

A short, smiling woman stood up from a chair, where she had been waiting. "You look like a Parker, so you must be Zack."

He looked at the woman again. "You have my grandpa's eyes," said Zack, " so you must be Ms. Dorothy." She laughed.

Zack's friends crowded through the door, and he introduced them.

Ms. Dorothy said, "I bet you boys are ready to hear some Indian stories."

She told them to come on in and sit on the bench. "I reckon I better start with Chief Quanah Parker, although his pa, Chief Peta Nacona, was pretty interesting too," she said.

Then the story began.

Chapter 7

MYSTERY CHIEF

Dorothy Parker's blue eyes danced with excitement as she recounted story after story about Chief Quanah Parker.

She told the boys of his hatred for the whites when his parents died, and how he led daring raids in Texas and Mexico for seven long years.

She explained how he was never caught by the U.S. Army until the buffalo were nearly gone and the Comanche people were starving.

The stories lasted for hours, but the time seemed to fly by. "In the last years of his life Quanah was a great diplomat," Ms. Dorothy continued. She told them that the chief had encouraged his people to adopt new ways. Finally, she stopped to draw a deep breath.

Zack stood up and ran out of the museum. "Hey, where are you going?" Josh yelled after him. Zack ran to the truck, reached inside the open window, and grabbed a brown grocery bag he had left on the seat.

The guys were standing in the doorway looking puzzled. Zack headed back into the museum, and they followed him into the room where Ms. Dorothy sat waiting.

Zack put the bag down and pulled a book out. Opening the book, where a candy bar wrapper marked the page, Zack turned the book toward Ms. Dorothy.

Pointing to the chief in the picture, he asked, "Is that Chief Quanah Parker?" He held his breath.

He waited while she looked carefully at the picture. He just knew she was going to say yes.

"No," she said.

"What?" he demanded. "Are you sure?"

"Quanah was taller and built more like his father, Peta Nocona," she commented, still looking at the book.

Zack dug into the sack again and pulled out the old family bibles. Ms. Dorothy gasped with delight, and taking them gently, she opened the one on the top. Inside was the old photo they had found in the attic.

"Speak of the devil!" she exclaimed holding up the old brown picture. "This is Chief Parker!"

Zack was puzzled. So the chief in his dreams was not Quanah Parker. Who could he be? And why was he after him?

Zack's hands felt damp, and he had a lump the size of a golf ball in his throat.

"Zack, are you okay?" Ms. Dorothy asked.

"No, I'm not okay," Zack said. Suddenly four pairs of eyes were staring at him.

"What's wrong?" Josh demanded.

Wes added, "Whatever it is, Zack, we can help you."

He stood, quietly gathering the nerve to tell the whole truth to his best friends. The problem was, he wasn't sure where to begin.

Seth put his hand on Zack's shoulder. "Does this have something to do with your sudden interest in Comanche Indians?" he asked gently.

Zack sat down and put his face in his hands. He was finally going to tell someone about the warrior. He decided to tell them about the dreams and see how they reacted.

"You're not going to believe me," he said.

Zack took a deep breath and told them about the terrifying dreams in all their vivid detail.

He told them about the dream where the horse almost stomped him to death, and then about the dream where he was shot with the warrior's arrow.

Seth looked uncomfortable and ran his finger inside the collar of his shirt. "Is there more?" he asked.

"Yes, there's more," Zack said. He hesitated. "After the horse dream, I woke up and my Gameboy had been pounded into dust right on my bedroom floor."

Then Zack told them about waking up in a bed full of blood. The wound was the same in his nightmare.

"No way!" exclaimed Josh.

"And one more thing," Zack said, "Doc is afraid to come into my room."

"I saw on TV that animals are supposed to be sensitive to ghosts," said Seth.

"Thanks for weirding us all out, dude," said Josh.

"Like Zack's story wasn't weird already," Seth replied.

"Zack do you think the warrior is a ghost?" Ms. Dorothy asked.

Zack stared at her. "Yes, I do. And I thought he was Chief Quanah Parker, but now I know he's not."

"Who is he?" asked Seth.

"I don't know," said Zack, "but I know that he's angry. And he seems to get angrier and more violent with each dream. That's why I'm telling you now. Because I'm afraid."

"Well, then. We'll just have to find out the identity of your mystery warrior," Ms. Dorothy said calmly. "Won't we?"

Chapter 8

COMANCHE MOON

The group quickly formed a plan to locate information on warriors that might be connected to Quanah Parker.

Ms. Dorothy would check with her museum contacts.

Seth would check out the Internet. Josh would ask the cowboys at his dad's ranch.

Wes would quiz Buck Thomas, the arrowhead expert, and Zack would enlist the help of Ms. Rhodes, the librarian.

Everyone agreed that they would meet again in two days in Llano and report on their findings.

The guys all piled into the truck and headed home. It was dark when they drove away from the museum. The truck was the only vehicle on the road. The moon blazed like a giant white dinner plate tossed into a black starry sky. The only sound was the occasional howling of a distant coyote.

Zack was still nervous about the nightmares. Thinking about them made his heart race.

"Hold on!" yelled Josh suddenly. The truck slid, and the stench of burning rubber filled the air. Josh yanked the steering wheel, trying to get control of the skittering truck.

Sitting in the middle of the road was a lone coyote. It never moved.

Josh's truck swerved off the road and stopped, just inches from an old barbed-wire fence. "Everyone okay?" Josh asked.

"Look at that," said Wes, pointing.

The coyote, his yellow eyes glowing, stared at them. The boys seemed unable to look away. Their eyes locked with the coyote's for what seemed like forever.

Then the beast slowly got up and walked away. It turned once, offering the boys one more warning glance before vanishing into the darkness at the side of the road.

"That is the oddest thing I have ever seen," Seth said.

"Spooky," said Wes.

"Normally a coyote avoids humans, unless it's starving," added Seth.

"That coyote looked fat enough to me," said Wes.

"It's a bad omen," Josh muttered.

"What do you mean?" Zack asked.

"The moon, the coyote, the whole thing. It ain't good, if you ask me," Josh said. "I heard that some Indians can change shape, so maybe that coyote was an Indian trying to tell us something."

Josh slowly pulled the truck back onto the dusty road. An hour later they were home.

Zack woke up early the next morning. His lights were still on. Stretching, he realized he had avoided another ghostly nightmare. He decided he'd try to sleep with the lights on every night.

After dressing quickly he quietly crossed the hall to the bathroom. He didn't want to wake his mom. Ten minutes later he got his bike out of the garage and rode to the Coffee Cup Cafe.

He went inside and ordered the breakfast special with scrambled eggs. The library opened at 9 a.m., so he should have plenty of time to talk to Ms. Rhodes before he had to work the afternoon shift at the drugstore.

He finished his breakfast and dug deep in his pocket for a wad of wrinkled dollar bills. After he pulled them apart to pay for his food, he started toward the door.

He overheard one of the old timers at the large center table say something about a "Comanche moon."

Zack spun around and walked over to the old men.

"Excuse me," he said.

"What can I do for you, young fella?" the oldest man said.

"What's a Comanche moon?" Zack asked.

The man leaned back, and patted his mouth with a napkin. "The Comanche used to conduct raids under the full moon," he said. "It was bright enough to guide them through the countryside. That's a Comanche moon."

"Their enemies sometimes called it a blood moon," another man added. "Some folks think it's a bad omen."

"Thanks," Zack said. Then he headed outside to his bike.

Riding over to the library, Zack thought about what Josh had said. He had called the moon a bad omen, too. Maybe he was right.

Zack bumped up the library steps on his bike just as the doors were unlocked.

Inside, he asked Ms. Rhodes about local Indian myths and legends that might include Chief Quanah Parker.

"I think I'll have to do a little research on that," she said. "Why don't you come back tomorrow?"

Zack spent the rest of the day at work. The drugstore was busy. He worked the soda fountain during lunch, and guessed that he made fifty cherry cokes in two hours.

On the way home, Zack made several phone calls on his cell phone. He tried Josh and left a message. Wes didn't answer either. Seth had apparently forgotten to charge his phone again.

Zack felt let down. He was hoping someone had news about the mystery chief.

His mom wasn't home yet, so he stretched out on the couch. The air conditioner made a gentle whirring sound. Zack looked at the ceiling fan swirling over his head and thought about his day.

The next thing he knew, something was tickling his face. It was the fuzzy throw blanket his mom kept on the back on the couch. He must have fallen asleep and pulled the blanket down while he was sleeping.

It was dark outside. He fell back asleep, but slept restlessly, waking up every hour. Finally, sometime after four in the morning, he fell into a deep sleep.

He dreamed of the day they had all been at the river. The day he cut his foot on the arrowhead.

He could see the guys, and they were all laughing. Then suddenly he felt a gust of wind. He was above the river looking down. The guys were gone.

Zack turned, and the ghost chief stood in front of him. The man's face was calm this time, not angry and twisted.

It was as if he could not see Zack, even though he was only inches away.

Zack took a step back. Just as he was about to turn and run, the ghost passed through him. Zack felt a violent chill. The boy turned to see the ghost continue making his way down to the river. He was wearing the bear claw necklace. When he reached the water he stopped and scanned the horizon.

Hoofbeats pounded through the air. A younger man was riding toward them. Zack recognized him right away. He had the same braided hair in the picture Zack found in the attic. He was Quanah Parker.

Quanah slid off the horse's back, and the two men began to talk quietly. The ghost chief seemed to be getting angry, his face was twisted. Suddenly both men were shouting, but Zack couldn't understand their strange words. Quanah kept saying "Nami, Nami."

The chief talked faster and louder and kept saying something about "Niatz."

They must be speaking in Comanche, thought Zack.

Quanah turned, and the ghost chief shouted something. Quanah lunged toward him, and the men began to fight.

They locked arms. Quanah was taller than his opponent. Still, the ghost chief threw Quanah back and jumped on him.

Then, with both hands tight around his neck, he started to choke Quanah.

They rolled around on the ground, and Quanah began choking the ghost chief.

The ghost chief clutched at the ground around him. His hand finally found a large rock and, raising it, he smashed Quanah in the head. Hard.

Quanah grunted and sagged lifelessly to the ground. The ghost chief stood up. He gazed down at Quanah's body and spit on him. Then the chief went to the river's edge. He knelt down to drink the cool water.

Zack's heart was racing. He figured he would be next.

Zzzzt! From behind him, an arrow whizzed toward its target, finding the center of the ghost chief's back.

A web of bright red blood spread out from the arrow as the ghost chief's arm reached around to pull it free. His arm dropped lifeless to his side. Then the chief fell face first into the river.

Something hit Zack. He grabbed his chest thinking it might be an arrow, but realized it was the coffee table. He had fallen off of the couch.

Chapter 9

PIECES OF THE PUZZLE

In the morning, Zack's cell phone rang. "Man, I think I got something for you!" exclaimed Josh. "Yesterday I spent the whole day out mending fences with Simms, Shuffle, and Chili. They told me something I think might help you."

Josh took a deep breath. "They told me that people used to say the river was haunted right by our swimming hole."

"Did they see the ghost?" Zack asked.

"No, but they heard stories about it, and people said the ghost was a Comanche Indian."

"Did he have an arrow in his back?" Zack asked.

Josh gasped. "How did you know?"

There was a pause while Zack formed a plan. "It's a long story, and I have to get to the library, so meet me at the cafe at noon," Zack said.

"You got it," Josh replied.

After talking to Josh, Zach decided to call Ms. Dorothy and see if she could meet them at the cafe.

"Yes, I'll be there, and I have something to show you!" she said mysteriously.

"Is it something you can tell me about now?" Zack asked.

"No, you need to see it. I'll see you at the cafe," she answered.

On the way to the library, Zack's cell phone began to vibrate in his pocket.

It was Seth, calling to tell him that he had been able to locate the name of an Indian expert, John Archer.

"Great!" Zack said.

"Not really, since he died a long time ago," Seth admitted.

"Not so great," said Zack. "Hey, can you look up something for me on your computer?"

He asked Seth to look up the two strange words he heard from the two Comanches, and to call Wes to tell him about the noon meeting at the cafe.

In a few minutes, Zack was facing Ms. Rhodes, who was looking at him over her giant library desk.

"Did you find any books for me about Indian legends or about Quanah Parker?" Zack asked quietly.

"Not exactly," Ms. Rhodes whispered back.

Zack gave her a confused look.

"I have the name of a book, which is no longer in print, that would meet all of your search requirements," she told him. "But it's rare, and you would have to find a book dealer that would have a copy."

She handed Zack a piece of paper. On the slip of paper she had written in her neat handwriting was *True Tales of Texas Indians* by John Archer.

John Archer? That was the same name as Seth's Indian expert.

Zack's cell phone began to jiggle in his pocket before he could even get on his bike.

"Hey, Wes," he said.

"I'm in the cafe, and I've got something to tell you," Wes said excitedly.

"You're thirty minutes early," Zack said glancing at his watch.

"I know, but Buck Thomas knew something about some ghosts at the river, so when are you getting your lazy butt over here?" Wes asked.

"Did you say ghosts?" Zack asked.

"Yeah, two of them," Wes answered.

"No way!" Zack exclaimed.

Zack arrived at the cafe three minutes later. He parked his bike and went inside. Wes stood up and waved from a table in the back of the tiny cafe.

"Buck Thomas said there's always been good arrowhead hunting where we swim, but nobody goes there because of the ghosts," Wes said before Zack could even sit down.

"Does one of them have an arrow in his back?" Zack asked.

Wes was stunned. "How did you know that?" he asked.

"Tell me about the other ghost," Zack said.

"Well, she has an arrow in her chest," Wes said slowly.

She?

Just then the bell on the door jangled as Seth arrived. Zack and Wes waved him over.

"Okay, I found out what your two words mean," Seth said. "They're Comanche words. *Nami* means sister, and *naitz* means no. Where did you hear those words, anyway?"

Just as Zack was about to answer, the bell jangled again, and Josh and Ms. Dorothy arrived. The two newcomers pushed through the lunch crowd and sat down at the table.

"I had another dream last night," Zack announced, looking around the table.

"Are you okay?" Ms. Dorothy asked, looking concerned.

"Tell us about it before we get started, and don't leave anything out," Seth demanded.

Zack described the fight by the river's edge in his dream. They all gasped at the part when the arrow shot the ghost chief.

"Unreal," Seth said.

"Freaky!" Wes exclaimed.

Zack asked, "Wes, do you think Quanah was talking about his sister?"

"She probably wasn't born yet," Seth said.

"What about the other ghost Buck told me about?" Wes asked.

"Ms. Rhodes told me about a book that might help us," Zack said.

Ms. Dorothy pulled a plastic bag out of her purse. "I have a book that might help us, too," she said. "One of my museum friends is a book collector." She put the book on the table, then went on, "The book he gave me is called *True Tales of Texas Indians*."

Zack couldn't believe it. "Is it by John Archer?" he asked.

Ms. Dorothy exclaimed, "Yes, it is!"

They looked in the index and found Quanah Parker listed in a chapter called "River Spirits." Ms. Dorothy read a story that was told by Quanah himself and passed down through his band until John Archer heard it and put it into his book.

Quanah told of his love for a Comanche girl whose brother was also a chief. Quanah had asked a medicine man to make a love charm that would cause the girl to come to him, but it didn't work.

Quanah went to a meeting place near a river to talk to the girl's brother.

Quanah had gone to the meeting place to offer horses as a wedding gift to the girl's brother. The brother was proud and jealous of Quanah, so he refused. Quanah got angry, and the two began to fight.

The brother knocked him out with a rock. When Quanah awoke he saw the brother dead in the river, shot by an arrow.

Quanah left him there and went to his horse to leave. He hadn't gone far when he found the girl with an arrow in her chest. She was barely alive, but told him that she had plunged the arrow in her own chest to punish herself for killing her brother.

With her last words she confessed to Quanah that she loved him so much she had killed her own brother to protect him.

Everyone at the table was silent.

Then Ms. Dorothy said, "That is one sad story."

The waitress brought their orders and, as they began to eat, Seth said, "The question is, why are you having these dreams and how can we get them to stop?"

Zack who was holding John Archer's book in his hand said, "At least the pieces of the puzzle are starting to come together."

Chapter 10

THE WARRIOR CHIEF

No one seemed to know what to do or say next about Zack's ghostly problem. Zack had his notes and the book. What he really needed was some quiet time to sort everything out. He told his friends he was going home to think. He promised to call them all if anything else happened.

Several hours passed, and Zack was sitting at the kitchen table. He had a spiral notebook, loose papers, and books spread out all around him.

He wondered if his mom was home yet. Zack looked in the direction of the back door.

His heart gave a painful thud and almost jumped out of his chest.

There stood the warrior chief. His dark eyes were filled with hatred. The bear claw necklace hung from his neck.

He lifted his hand to his neck and slowly made a cutting gesture with his finger. Then he pointed at Zack.

Zack was filled with fear. This felt different than the other dreams. He slapped himself hard in the face, trying to shock himself out of the nightmare.

Then he realized that he wasn't dreaming. He was wide awake.

The chief began to laugh like a crazy man. Then he took a few steps forward.

Zack jumped to his feet and looked at the chief. "What do you want from me?" he asked, trying to sound brave. The chief turned slightly, and Zack could see the shaft of the arrow sticking in his back. Terrified, Zack turned to run, and the chief came after him with a loud cry.

Zack ran toward the hallway with the chief close behind him. He turned into his room, slammed the door, and locked it. He moved to the other side of the room and tried to catch his breath. The chief stepped right through the locked door, laughing wildly.

I am so stupid, Zack thought. Now what? "Why me?" he shouted at the chief.

The chief grabbed Zack's arm. Zack pulled away rolling to the side. The ghost jumped on him. Then he snatched a big handful of Zack's hair and slammed his head into the corner of the desk.

Zack felt woozy. Some drops of blood tricked into his eye. He reached up to touch the gash on his forehead.

Then he felt the chief's fingers around his neck. They were freezing cold, so cold they seemed to burn his skin. They began to crush his throat.

I need air, Zack thought. He was pulling and clawing at the chief's arms.

The chief had supernatural strength. Zack's eyes were bulging out and rainbows were swirling around his room. He saw another shadow rise up in front of him.

"Dad?" Zack said.

"Dude!" He thought he heard Josh shouting. "Dude!"

Then everything went black.

Chapter 11

TEN BEARS

Zack felt someone shaking him. He rolled to his side, coughing hard. Josh was sitting beside him. His eyes were huge, and his skin was pale. "Are you okay?" Josh asked.

Zack reached up to touch his throat and flinched. He could hardly swallow. Josh explained that the ghost had vanished the minute he had shouted, but not before he had seen him choking Zack.

"Dead," Zack said pointing to himself.

"Yep, he wanted you dead," Josh said.

Josh pulled out his cell phone and called Wes. He told him what had happened and asked him to get over to Zack's house.

While they waited, Josh told Zack that he had stopped by to tell him some news. One of the cowboys knew a medicine man. Zack nodded his head again and looked a little relieved.

Wes arrived and ran into Zack's room. He looked at the red marks on Zack's neck. "It has to be revenge," Wes said.

Josh looked as if a light bulb had suddenly flipped on in his mind. "That's it! The chief thinks Quanah killed him because he never saw his sister!" Josh exclaimed. "And you're Quanah's living relative."

"Can you make it out to the ranch?" Josh asked Zack.

Zack nodded weakly.

Fifteen minutes later they picked up Seth and then headed out of town on the dusty road that led to the ranch.

A ranch hand named Simms was waiting at the bunkhouse. He had called his medicine man friend, Ten Bears, to the ranch.

Ten Bears filled the doorway like a young giant. He was wearing blue jeans and a baseball cap.

In a painful whisper, Zack explained his problem.

"You are in great danger," Ten Bears said.

A few cowboys gathered around the table as Ten Bears asked Zack questions.

Then Ten Bears stood up and walked around the room. He thought for a moment and chose his words carefully.

"The warrior in your dreams cannot rest. He died not from the arrow but from the river," he said. He explained that the Comanche believe that souls who drown cannot rest.

The way the warrior died and his belief that Quanah had killed him were the cause of the vengeful spirit.

Josh said, "I think we pretty much figured that out already, man."

Wes asked, "Can we kill the spirit?"

"No. Hatred makes the spirit very strong," Ten Bears said. "But there is a way to stop the spirit from attacking you."

"How?" Zack asked softly. The others barely heard him speak.

"It may be difficult," Ten Bears admitted. "You will need something that belonged to the warrior's spirit."

"The arrowhead!" Wes exclaimed.

"What about the bear claw?" Seth asked.

"The more things you have, the better," Ten Bears said.

Zack pulled the arrowhead out of his pants pocket. Josh and Wes left for Zack's house to retrieve the bear claw.

Ten Bears explained that the old Comanche often buried their dead in caves or crevices. After the burial they would pray and fast for three days.

Zack, Seth, and the cowboys watched as Ten Bears laid out a small patch of buckskin.

He painted a few tiny symbols on it with a marker. Then he covered the other side with a fine powder.

"Can you make him go away by giving him a proper burial?" Zack asked quietly.

Ten Bears looked surprised by Zack's question.

"No, I cannot," Ten Bears said. He pointed at Zack. "But you can."

Zack looked horrified. "I have to do it? By myself?" he asked.

Ten Bears replied, "I have done all I can. Besides, you are the youngest man in your family. The bad blood is between your families now. You must make things right with the spirit because you are the descendant of Quanah."

He told Zack to find a holy place to put the warrior's spirit in its final resting place.

Then he gave instructions for wrapping the claw and the arrowhead in the buckskin, and making it into a small pouch.

"You must do this soon, or the warrior's spirit will kill you," Ten Bears warned. Then he left.

The cowboys were all silent when Josh and Wes came in with the bear claw jar.

"Where did Ten Bears go?" Wes asked.

"He's done," said Seth grimly. "It's all up to Zack now."

Chapter 12

ENCHANTED ROCK

Zack called his mom and told her he would be camping at the ranch with his friends for a few days. He hated to lie, but he didn't want her to be scared.

That night they all slept in the bunkhouse. In the morning, Wes gently shook Zack awake. "We've got everything packed," he told Zack.

"Where are we going to take the remains?" Josh asked.

Zack had a feeling that Ms. Dorothy would know the right place.

He asked Seth to call her and explain what had happened. His throat was still pretty sore.

After Seth hung up, he told them Zack was right.

"Ms. Dorothy says we should take the remains to a place called Enchanted Rock," he said. "She gave me directions. She's going to meet us out there."

Heading west out of town, they saw a large brown sign for a right turn that said it was twelve miles to Enchanted Rock.

They were at the entrance gate fifteen minutes later.

A large rock formation jutted into the sky. It was really a small mountain, and it was the color of dried blood.

People said it was haunted because sometimes, at night, it sounded like it was crying. Seth said the mineral content and air temperature caused the wailing. Zack agreed that it was a good place for a spirit to rest.

Ms. Dorothy was waiting at the gate with three large containers of water and a box of crackers. She handed them off to the boys, and said, "Watch out for snakes, be sure you are serious or this may not work, and call me as soon as you are free of the spirit."

She hugged Zack, and then turned to leave. The boys gathered their sleeping bags, gear, and backpacks. They moved along the path that led to Enchanted Rock. Soon they were halfway up a rocky slope, and the climb began to get steep.

Wes said, "I hope it doesn't get any harder to climb. We didn't bring any climbing equipment."

"Let's start looking for a good place to put this stuff," Zack said.

When they were almost at the top, they stopped to rest. They had climbed so high they could see for miles.

Zack noticed a wide crack that ran down the side of the Enchanted Rock.

He walked over and knelt down, and carefully placed the buckskin pouch from Ten Bears in the crack.

Then the boys formed a circle on the top of Enchanted Rock, and together said the words of the Indian prayer that Ten Bears had given them.

For three days they sat on the top of the mountain. They took turns sleeping, so they could follow Ten Bears's instructions. They had only the water and crackers Ms. Dorothy had given them for food.

On the third night, the full Comanche Moon was gone. Their campsite was nearly pitch black, especially when the moon passed behind the clouds.

Zack felt cold, and stirred in his sleep. As he turned on his side, an arm reached around from behind him, grabbed him by the neck, and began dragging him away from the campfire.

Where was the ghost taking him? Zack couldn't see much, but judging from the direction they were heading, they must be getting close to the edge of the mountain. Zack tried to yell, but couldn't get enough air.

He tried to grab something, anything, but all he felt was the rocky surface of the mountain. In sheer panic, he began to kick at the ground as he slid closer to the mountain's edge in the grip of the ghost.

Unknown to Zack, Josh was close behind. He had woken up and seen the ghost drag Zack away.

Josh knew the ghost was getting near the edge of the mountain, but he didn't know what he could do to stop the ghost from killing his friend. He tried to loop around and get between Zack and the ledge.

Zack couldn't see Josh. He was thinking of the climb up Enchanted Rock and how the ground had looked as if it were miles below them. He imagined himself falling from the top.

Then both Zack and Josh heard a voice, the soft voice of a woman. They couldn't understand her words. She began to beg, and then to weep, and then, miraculously, the powerful arm around Zack's neck let go.

Then they heard the deep voice of a man.

The pale moon slipped from behind the clouds and silvery beams of light covered the top of the mountain.

Zack could see Josh standing near the side of the mountain. Between them stood the warrior spirit. He was comforting the young woman, who was sobbing loudly.

Zack looked at the woman in surprise. It must be the warrior's sister. The warrior turned and looked at Zack. His face seemed calm now, not angry.

Zack felt a strange surge of peace. The warrior must know the truth about his death. His sister must have told him.

Josh walked over to Zack and pulled him to his feet. A strong gust of wind blew in their faces and then suddenly stopped. The spirits had vanished, leaving only a chill that crept up Zack's spine.

REST IN PEACE

Zack awoke with a jolt. He sat up in bed. His heart was racing.

He looked around the room. Everything was just as it should be. Doc lay snoring on the floor. Zack leaned over and rubbed the dog's ears.

Sleepily, he said, "Good boy, Doc."

It had been a week since they had taken the buckskin pouch to Enchanted Rock.

The first thing they had done after coming down from the rock that night was call Ms. Dorothy. Later that evening, he and Ms. Dorothy had explained everything to his mom, who kept hugging Zack the entire time and, once he had gone to bed, checked on him every hour all night long.

Zack told her not to worry. No more nightmares, no more warrior nights.

He was finally able to rest in peace.

ABOUT THE AUTHOR

Marci Bales Peschke was born in Indiana, grew up in Florida, and now lives in Texas. She has lived in three haunted houses, but now lives with her husband, two children, and a feisty black and white cat named Phoebe. She is an official member of the Scottish Clan MacIntyre. She loves reading, watching movies, and having tea parties.

ABOUT THE ILLUSTRATOR

Brann Garvey grew up in the great state of Iowa, where he studied art and visual communications. He graduated from the Minneapolis College of Art & Design with a degree in illustration. Brann is usually found with one or more of the following: a pencil in his hand, a comic book, a remote for watching DVDs, or his pet kitty, Iggy.

GLOSSARY

aggressive (uh-GRESS-iv)—fierce or threatening behavior

bareback (BAIR-bak)—riding a horse without a saddle

buckskin (BUHK-skin)—a strong, soft material made from the skin of a deer

civilization (siv-uh-luh-ZAY-shuhn)—an organized society

formation (for-MAY-shuhn)—a pattern or a shape

mesquite (mess-SKEET)—a small spiny shrub native to Mexico and the Southwest United States

salve (SAV)—a cream that relieves pain and helps heal wounds, burns, and sores

DISCUSSION QUESTIONS

1. What was the scariest nightmare Zack had? Why do you think it was the scariest?

2. Do you think this story could really happen? Why or why not?

3. Do you believe in ghosts after reading the story? Why or why not?

4. Why do you think Zack and his friends did research on the ghost in Zack's nightmares?

WRITING PROMPTS

1. Zack was haunted because of something that happened to his family in the past. Do you know much about your own family's past? If you could travel in time, is there a relative you'd want to visit? Maybe a relative in a different country? Tell us about your time-travel trip.

2. If one of your friends told you that they were haunted, or had seen a ghost, would you believe them? What sort of advice would you give?

3. Zack and his friends spent several days and nights on Enchanted Rock. If you had been with them, how would you feel about your time there? Describe how you spent those three days.

ALSO PUBLISHED BY STONE ARCH BOOKS

The Curse of the Wendigo
by Scott R. Welvaert

Agate and Buck set out on a spine-tingling adventure through the haunted Canadian woods to track down their missing parents. But an ancient curse means that Buck and Agate are being hunted, too.

The Pirate, Big Fist, and Me
by M. J. Cosson

When Levi Viggers the Eighth is sentenced to an entire year of after-school detention, he comes across a book with some family secrets. Unfortunately, his bully cousin knows the same riddles exist.

Missing
by M. Sobel Spirn

Sam's constant lying makes it hard for people to believe him when his dad is kidnapped. With the help of his friend, Josh, Sam gets closer to the truth — and to danger.

Rock Art Rebel
by M. J. Cosson

Beto's urban art is labeled graffiti by the police, so he spends the summer with his faraway relatives. Then Beto discovers ancient art in an unexpected place, and he's the only one who can save it.

INTERNET SITES

Do you want to know more about subjects related to this book? Or are you interested in learning about other topics? Then check out FactHound, a fun, easy way to find Internet sites.

Our investigative staff has already sniffed out great sites for you!

Here's how to use FactHound:

1. Visit *www.facthound.com*

2. Select your grade level.

3. To learn more about subjects related to this book, type in the book's ISBN number: **1598890719**.

4. Click the **Fetch It** button.

FactHound will fetch the best Internet sites for you!